Seraph of the End

VAMPIRE REIGN

4

D0553521

STORY BY Takaya Kagami
ART BY Yamato Yamamoto
STORYBOARDS BY Daisuke Furuya

CHARACTERS

GUREN ICHINOSE

Lieutenant Colonel of the Moon Demon Company, a Vampire Extermination Unit. He recruited Yuichiro into the Japanese Imperial Demon Army.

YUICHIRO HYAKUYA

A boy who escaped from the vampire capital, he has both great kindness and a great desire for revenge. Lone wolf.

SHIHO KIMIZUKI

Yuichiro's friend.
Smart but abrasive.

YOICHI SAOTOME

Yuichiro's friend.
His sister was killed by a vampire.

MITSUBA SANGU

An elite soldier who has been part of the Moon Demon Company since age 13. Bossy.

SHINOA HIRAGI

Guren's subordinate and Yuichiro's surveillance officer. Member of the illustrious Hiragi family.

STORY

A mysterious virus decimates the human population, and vampires claim dominion over the world. Yuichiro and his adopted family of orphans are kept as vampire fodder in an underground city until the day Mikaela, Yuichiro's best friend, plots an ill-fated escape for the orphans. Only Yuichiro survives and reaches the surface.

Four years later, Yuichiro enters into the Moon Demon Company, a Vampire Extermination Unit in the Japanese Imperial Demon Army, to enact his revenge. It is there he gains Asuramaru, a demon-possessed weapon capable of killing vampires.

Along with his squad mates Shinoa, Yoichi, Kimizuki and Mitsuba, Yuichiro deploys to Shinjuku with orders to thwart a vampire attack. However, in the battle he spots someone who looks a lot like Mika...

Seraph of the End
VAMPIRE REIGN

MIKAELA HYAKUYA

Yuichiro's best friend. He was supposedly killed but has come back to life as a vampire.

FERID BATHORY

A Seventh Progenitor vampire, he killed Mikaela.

KRUL TEPES

Queen of the Vampires and a Third Progenitor.

Seraph of the End

VAMPIRE REIGN

4

CONTENTS

CHAPTER 12
A Very Safe Supplement 005

CHAPTER 13
Reunion of Childhood Friends 051

CHAPTER 14
Everyone's a Sinner 099

CHAPTER 15
Complicated Connections 147

Four Years Ago

CHAPTER 12 **A Very Safe Supplement**

HEY...
WHAT IF SOMEDAY WE ESCAPE THE VAMPIRE CITY?
WHAT KIND OF STUFF WOULD YOU WANT TO DO THEN?
HUH?
THAT'S NON-SENSE, STUPID.
THE OUTSIDE WORLD IS DEAD. THE VIRUS KILLED EVERY-BODY.
WE'D NEVER GET OUT—
"What if," Yu! Just "what if."
WHAT IF ONE DAY JUST THE HYAKUYA ORPHANAGE FAMILY GOT OUT?
WHAT IF WE FOUND A WORLD WITH NO VAMPIRES IN IT AT ALL?
WOULDN'T THAT BE GREAT?

JUST US?
...
baf
smile
REALLY?
WELL... YEAH, THAT WOULD BE KINDA COOL, I GUESS.
YEP! JUST US AND OUR FAMILY.
WELL THEN...
I GUESS I MIGHT TRY A LITTLE HARDER AFTER ALL.
IT DIDN'T TURN OUT THAT WAY.
BUT ...
NOTHING!
HUH?

CHAPTER 12

A Very Safe Supplement

FOUR YEARS HAVE PASSED SINCE THEN.
BUT MIKA...

THE OUTSIDE WORLD ISN'T PARADISE.
WSH
DIE, HUMAN SCUM!
IT'S CRAWLING WITH THE BLOODSUCKERS THAT KILLED YOU.
SWAK

SHUT IT, VAMPIRE.
YOU'RE THE ONES WHO ARE GONNA DIE.
TAK
HEY!
WE'VE GOTTA HEAD ELSE-WHERE!
WE COULD STAY HERE OFFING VAMPIRES ALL DAY, BUT IT WON'T HELP ANYTHING!
I AGREE.
LT. COLONEL GUREN'S ORDERS WERE TO MEET HIM AT SHINJUKU'S 5TH STREET INTERSECTION ...
...AND TAKE OUT THE ENEMY'S LEADER!
YU-ICHIRO!

YUICHIRO? LET'S GO.
RIGHT, LET'S MOVE!
DMP

OH! ONE THING BEFORE WE REACH THE FRONT LINES.
DO YOU MIND, YUICHIRO?
HUH?
MIND WHAT?
I KNOW THIS IS SUDDEN...
...BUT LET'S BEGIN YOUR VERY FIRST TRAINING SESSION!♪
WHA...?
TRAINING SESSION ?

NO, DON'T STOP RUNNING.
I SHALL EXPLAIN ON OUR WAY.
IT'S PRECISELY BECAUSE WE'RE IN THE MIDDLE OF "ALL THIS."
BUT NOW? IN THE MIDDLE OF ALL THIS?
I'M SURE I NEEDN'T REMIND YOU AFTER WE FACED THAT VAMPIRE NOBLE IN THE STREETS NOT LONG AGO.
EVEN THOUGH YOU BEAR A WEAPON IN THE TOP RANK OF CURSED GEAR...
...A RARE "BLACK DEMON SERIES" SWORD...
...YOU COULD STILL BE KILLED IN THE BLINK OF AN EYE.
YOU'LL BE USELESS ON THE FRONT LINES.

AHA HA!
ANYWAY, ALL JOKING ASIDE.
I GET THE POINT!!
As helpful as a turd laying forgotten on the ground...
Completely useless.
Ha ha ha ha ha
WE DON'T HAVE TIME TO MESS AROUND.
SO, WHAT'S THE TRAINING?
IT ISN'T MUCH, REALLY.
THIS IS A FAIRLY TYPICAL SITUATION.
I'LL DO WHATEVER IT TAKES IF IT MEANS I CAN KILL MORE BLOOD-SUCKERS!
WHAT YOU'LL DO IS QUITE SIMPLE.
TAKE ONE OF THESE.
CHI-K

PILLS?
...

YES. THIS IS PRESENTLY THE MOST ADVANCED TRAINING METHOD AVAILABLE ...
DRUGGING UP.

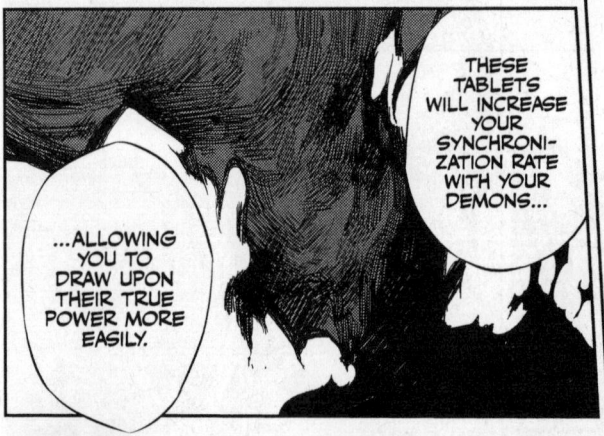
THESE TABLETS WILL INCREASE YOUR SYNCHRONI-ZATION RATE WITH YOUR DEMONS...
...ALLOWING YOU TO DRAW UPON THEIR TRUE POWER MORE EASILY.

IN THEORY ...
...ONE TABLET INCREASES YOUR POWER TO 150 PERCENT.
TWO WILL PUSH IT AS FAR UP AS 180 PERCENT.

SO I'LL BE ABLE TO FIGHT NOBLES?
WELL...
YOU WON'T DIE INSTANTLY AT LEAST.

HOWEVER, AFTER THE THIRD TABLET, ALL OF YOUR INTERNAL ORGANS WOULD RUPTURE.
MAN, IF I TOOK TEN OF THOSE THINGS ...!!
REALLY ?!
Aha ha! You'd be able to take on a god.
NOT ONLY THAT, THE TABLET'S EFFECTS LAST ONLY 15 MINUTES.
WHAT?
ASSUMING, OF COURSE, THE DAMAGE FROM THE SECOND TABLET HADN'T ALREADY SENT YOU INTO SHOCK.
ONCE IT WEARS OFF, YOU ARE FORCED OUT OF SYNC WITH YOUR DEMON...
... RENDERING YOU UTTERLY DEFENSE-LESS.
THAT IS WHERE THIS COMES IN.
THE MOST ANYONE USUALLY TAKES IS ONE.

WHAT'S THAT?
AN ALARM.
CLICK THE BUTTON AT THE TOP AND IT WILL RING 13 MINUTES LATER.
WHEN YOU HEAR IT, RUN.

BECAUSE TWO MINUTES LATER, YOU'LL BE A NORMAL HUMAN.
15−13=
...
UH, I'VE GOT A QUESTION.
YES?

IT TAKES TEN SECONDS FOR THE SUPPLEMENT TO TAKE EFFECT.
IN THOSE TEN SECONDS...

YOU DIDN'T GIVE THESE TO US WHEN WE FOUGHT THAT NOBLE.
WHY NOT?
WE STILL COULD NOT HAVE WON.
IF WE'D HAD THESE THEN—

RIGHT, OKAY.
ANOTHER QUESTION.
MY, YOU'RE INQUISITIVE TODAY.
ARE THESE PILLS WHAT YOU WERE TALKING ABOUT BEFORE?
THE WAY TO USE THE "TRUE POWER" OF OUR CURSED GEAR?
Ch, ch
WILL TAKING JUST ONE OF THESE ...
...FINALLY LET ME GET EVERYTHING OUT OF MY SWORD?
...
HE WOULD HAVE KILLED US ALL.

GETTING THE FULLEST OUT OF YOUR CURSED GEAR REQUIRES COPIOUS STUDY AND TRAINING.
NO.
THESE ARE A TEMPORARY MEASURE.
BUT LOOK AT THE WORLD AROUND US.
WE SIMPLY DON'T HAVE THE TIME FOR THAT.
THIS IS WAR.
FOR SURE.

GEEZ, DO YOU ALWAYS HAVE TO HARP ON THAT?
Ex-cuse me?
You say some-thing?
Guys ...
THE DRUGS ARE MEANT TO MAKE UP FOR THAT WHICH EVEN THE MOST DEVOTED TRAINING CAN'T PROVIDE.
WAR HAS ALREADY BEGUN.
STILL, I'M NOT SURE WHAT I THINK OF THIS.
RELYING ON PILLS AND ALL.
OH, DON'T WORRY.

THE DEMON ARMY ITSELF...
...ONE HUNDRED PERCENT GUARANTEES THAT THESE SUPPLEMENTS ARE POSITIVELY RIDDLED WITH HARMFUL SIDE EFFECTS.
THERE'S NOTHING "OKAY" ABOUT THAT!!
AHA HA!
WELL, IT DOES MAKE ONE NOT WANT TO RELY ON THEM.
BUT RIGHT NOW WE HAVEN'T GOT A CHOICE, SO EVERYBODY TAKE A PACKET.
...
CHIK
SO?
WHAT'S OUR TIMING FOR TAKING THESE THINGS?
TYPICALLY, THE COMMANDING OFFICER GIVES THE ORDER.
AND MOST DON'T RESORT TO IT UNLESS THEY'RE FACING A NOBLE.

LT. COLONEL GUREN WILL BE THE RANKING OFFICER AT THE BATTLEFIELD.
YOU'RE OUR SQUAD LEADER.
THEN YOU'LL TELL US WHEN, SHINOA?
THE RESPONSIBILITY FALLS TO HIM. I SUGGEST YOU ALL LISTEN TO HIS ORDERS.
THOUGH IF HE IS, AH...TOO PREOCCUPIED, I'LL GIVE THE ORDER IN HIS STEAD.
Front Lines

Shinjuku 5th Street Intersection

KA
NG
SHI
NG
DMP
DMP
TUP
TUP

KLANG
KLANG
KLANG
UNP
H

OH HO!
YOU'RE A STRONG ONE!
REALLY?
I DON'T THINK YOU'RE VERY GOOD, MYSELF.
REALLY, NOW.

WHO
SH
tap
EXPLODE.

FUDO MYO-O SPELL.
BOOM
TIP
TCH.
YOU MANAGED TO DODGE THAT?
YOU'VE GOTTA BE KIDDING ME.
THE EXPLOSION'S TRIGGER WAS TOO SLOW.
BESIDES, WHAT MADE YOU THINK ANCIENT SPELLS LIKE THAT WOULD WORK ON A VAMPIRE?
OOH!

YOUR POWER AND ARRO-GANCE ARE OVER-WHELM-ING.
SUCH A PERFOR-MANCE FROM YOU, MIKA.
BUT THAT ARROGANCE WILL TRIP YOU UP.
IT IS NO WONDER YOU ARE THIRD PROGENITOR KRUL TEPES'S FAVORITE.
SHALL I HELP YOU OUT?

WHY WOULD YOU IMPLY...
...THAT I'M EVEN REMOTELY LOSING?
AS I SAID, THEY ARE *TRIPPING* YOU.
LOOK. THEY NEVER INTENDED TO FIGHT ONE-ON-ONE.
THEY'VE SPOTTED IT, SHIGURE.
?!
NOW.

YES, SIR.
TWANG

tug
BOO
SH

THMM THMM THMM
GOSHI.
START THE ILLUSION.
ALREADY ON IT.

OVER HERE.
CHECKMATE, VAMPIRE.
...!!
TUP
HMPH.

NO
HAVE
You owe me one, Mika dear.
WHISH

WHMP
SKSHHHHHHH
WHAM
!!
SKSHHHH
WHOA. CRAP.
THEY'RE A LOT BETTER THAN WE EXPECTED.
GUREN!

ESPECIALLY THAT LONG-HAIRED ONE. HE'S INSANELY POWERFUL.
SEE, MIKA? YOU SHOULDN'T UNDER-ESTIMATE HUMANS.
THEY ARE GREEDY COWARDS, BUT ALSO EXCEPTIONALLY DETERMINED.
Ha ha! Though I'm sure I needn't tell that to a former human!
SHUT UP.
HEE.
ANY-WAY...
IT IS TIME WE TOOK THIS FIGHT SERIOUSLY.
IF WE WORK TOGETHER—
I'VE GOT IT COVERED NOW.
I KNOW THE WAY THEY WORK.
SWORD.
DRINK MORE OF MY BLOOD.

HEH HEH HEH.
OH, SUCH ARRO-GANCE.
I WONDER, IS THAT A LINGERING REMNANT OF BEING HUMAN?
...
THIS IS LOOKING LIKE IT MIGHT BE A TWO-TABLET KIND OF DAY.
EITHER THAT OR WE GIVE UP SHINJUKU AND RETREAT.
OR MAYBE...
Chik
YU'S SQUAD AND THEIR BLACK DEMON SERIES WEAPONS WILL GET HERE IN TIME.
YOU MUSTN'T!

LT. COLONEL!
THERE'S A GOOD CHANCE I'LL DIE EVEN IF I DON'T.
AS IT STANDS ...
...WE ONLY HAVE EIGHT MINUTES BEFORE THE SUPPLEMENT'S EFFECTS WEAR OFF.
WE HAVE TO TAKE THOSE TWO OUT INSIDE THAT TIME LIMIT.
TAKING A SECOND TABLET MIGHT KILL YOU!
THANKS FOR YOUR PATIENCE.
MIND IF I ASK YOU TO WAIT JUST A BIT LONGER THOUGH?
HOW MUCH LONGER?
ARE YOU DONE TALKING?
THEN LET'S GET STARTED.
IT'S TIME FOR US TO TAKE OUR MEDICINE, SEE.
DO YOU MIND GIVING US, OH... ANOTHER 20 SECONDS OR SO?
SKCH

HEH. GUESS NOT.
NOT ONLY THAT...
IS IT ME, OR HAVE YOU GOTTEN FASTER?
I DECIDED TO STOP HOLDING BACK.
HOLDING BACK IN BATTLE?! AREN'T YOU THE NAÏVE LITTLE BRAT.

KING
!!
THAT "LITTLE BRAT" IS ABOUT TO KILL YOU.
WHOA!
CRAP.
SHF
AM I REALLY GONNA DIE...?
WELL DAMN.

Hmm? I spy enemy reinforcements incoming.
I'd hurry up and finish him if I were you, Mika.

POP
EVERYONE, TAKE YOUR SUPPLEMENT NOW!
THE LT. COLONEL IS IN TROUBLE!
RESCUE THE LT. COLONEL AND THEN RETREAT IMMEDIATELY!
WHAP

LET'S GO!
RIGHT WITH YOU!
ZOOM
HMPH.
YOU DIE HERE, HUMAN.
shff
SCREW YOU.
GUREN !!

WHA
...?

MORE HUMANS ?
WHAT A PAIN IN THE—
WHAT ARE YOU DOING TO GUREN?!
Y...
YU...?

DIE, BLOOD-SUCKER ...

HUH?

Seraph of the End

VAMPIRE REIGN

Chapter 13
Reunion of Childhood Friends

Seraph of the End

VAMPIRE REIGN

NO...
Y...
YU?

NGK ....!
YU, WHAT ARE YOU DOING ?!
RUN THIS VAMPIRE THROUGH WITH YOUR CURSED GEAR! NOW!
SW
I CAN'T PULL MY SWORD OUT!
HA HA!
I WIN, VAMPIRE!

NGH!
SWSH
ZWS
SASH
...
THAT'S ...

SMAK

HUH?
I...
UM...

WHAT THE HELL WERE YOU DOING ?!
WHY DIDN'T YOU KILL IT WHEN YOU HAD THE CHANCE?!

KOFF

SHOVE

HUH?! H-HEY, ARE YOU OKAY?!
SLUMP

THIS IS A BATTLE-FIELD! STAY ALERT!
DON'T WORRY ABOUT ME, YOU LITTLE FOOL!

WHAT WERE YOU THINK-ING?!
HEY, IDIOT!

R-RIGHT ...

...

YUICHIRO, IS SOME-THING WRONG?

YEAH! YOU COULD HAVE KILLED THAT VAMPIRE!
WHY DIDN'T YOU ACTIVATE YOUR CURSED GEAR AND DESTROY IT?

MIKA'S MY FAMILY...

HE'S WITH THE VAMPIRES!

Aha!
That was Yuichiro Hyakuya, wasn't it?
So what will you do now, Mika?
What a touching reunion.
I'm so moved I could almost cry!
It seems obvious to me...
...that little Yu is being *used* by those humans.
I'm going to save him, of course.

A HUMAN COULD NEVER BE ONE OF US.
BUT HE'S A HUMAN TOO, YOU KNOW.
YES.
FROM THOSE UGLY, GREEDY HUMANS?
OH, BUT I KNOW!
Paff
LAY ONE HAND ON HIM...
...AND I WILL KILL YOU.
AS KRUL DID TO YOU...
...I COULD DO FOR HIM. MAKE HIM A VAM—
SPAB

HOW UNUSUAL FOR YOU TO BE SO VEHEMENT.
IT WAS JUST A LITTLE JOKE, MIKA.
Ана на на!
I WILL KEEP THE OTHER HUMANS OCCUPIED ...
HERE, LET ME GIVE YOU A HAND.
AH WELL.
...WHILE YOU GO RESCUE YOUR BELOVED PRINCESS.
...

OF COURSE HE DID. HE'S NICE.

YU FOUND FRIENDS.

...THEY'LL DECEIVE HIM.

BUT BECAUSE HE'S TOO NICE...

THEY'RE JUST PRETENDING TO BE HIS FRIENDS...

HUMANS WILL USE HIM.

HUMANS ARE GREEDY...
YU.

...

HEY !!
IS THAT YOU, MIKA?!

MIKA...
MIKA...!!
SO IT'S REALLY YOU...!
Y...
YU...

WELL THEN, SHALL WE BEGIN?
ALL HUMANS BESIDES PRECIOUS LITTLE YU MUST DIE.
GOOD-NESS.
WHAT AN UTTERLY ADORABLE REACTION.
NO WONDER YOU ARE SO ATTACHED TO HIM.
!
I HEARD YOU WERE LOOKING FOR ME...
... SEVENTH PRO-GENITOR.

WE DON'T NEED TO KILL THE HUMANS NOW.
WITH YOU HERE, IT IS GAME, SET, MATCH.
Aah, Crowley!
You kept me waiting.
WE'LL TRANSITION THEM FROM "VAMPIRE EXTERMINATION UNIT" TO "VAMPIRE LIVESTOCK."
INSTEAD, LET US MAKE THEM OUR CATTLE.
CHING
EVERYONE, FEEL FREE TO SAMPLE THEIR BLOOD.
MORE NOBLES.
DAMN.

EVERYONE PREPARE TO RETREAT!
HUH?
WE HAVE TO ABANDON SHINJUKU.
TRYING TO TAKE OUT THEIR LEADER TOOK TOO LONG.
THAT'S IT FOR US.
WE CAN'T RETREAT YET!
THEY STILL HAVE MY FAMILY!
MIKA'S STILL OVER THERE!
WAIT, HOLD ON!
YU-ICHIRO ...
WHAT, SO YOU'D RATHER WE ALL STAY HERE AND DIE?

RIGHT NOW, WE REALLY SHOULDN'T ...
HOLD RANKS AND MOVE BACK TOWARD THE WALLS!
RETREAT !!
WSH
!!
RGH!
YOU WON'T GET AWAY THAT EASILY.

SWOOSH
YAH !!
URK!
OOH, you're quick.
BUT STILL TOO YOUNG.

FWP
WHOK
ZWIP
AND YOUR BLADE, SIR LION...
...HAS SLOWED NOW THAT YOU'RE WOUNDED.
!!
GUREN !!

LET'S SEE HOW YOU TASTE...
Patf
SLURCH

SPLAT
SPLAT
WHAP
Aha.
It was just a little joke, Mika.
No need to get so mad.
MIKA...

YU...
FORGET ALL OF THEM AND RUN AWAY WITH ME!
HUH?
RUN? I-I CAN'T...
COME ON!
DWAH ?!

HUP
YU-ICHIRO!
SOON
!!

H-HEY! MIKA, CUT IT OUT!
WHAT ARE YOU DOING ?!
YOU CAN'T STAY THERE, YU. IT'S A BAD PLACE!

I SAID STOP!!
SHOVE
AH!

DMP

THOSE HUMANS ARE USING YOU.
YOU HAVE TO—
WHAT-EVER, JUST STOP A SECOND!
WHAT'RE YOU TALKING ABOUT ?!

...
"THOSE HUMANS" ARE USING ME?

WHAT'S THAT MEAN, MIKA?
YOU...

YOU MAKE IT SOUND...
...LIKE YOU AREN'T HUMAN ANYMORE.

IT'S MY FAULT, ISN'T IT?
MY FAULT FOR RUN-NING AWAY...

C'MON, WE HAVE TO GO.
IT'S TOO DAN-GEROUS HERE.
NO!
IT'S NOT YOUR FAULT!!

HI, YU!
YU.
AS OF TODAY, WE'RE FAMILY.
I'M MIKAELA HYAKUYA.
MIKA, I...I CAN'T.
I CAN'T LEAVE.
I HAVE FRIENDS BACK THERE...
PLEASE.
I WON'T TRY TO DECEIVE YOU!
THOSE HUMANS ARE ONLY TRYING TO USE—
I'M YOUR ONLY TRUE FRIEND!
NO, YOU DON'T!

EEEEEEK!!
?!
THAT WAS SHINOA'S VOICE!
GRAB
PLEASE, YU! DON'T LOOK BACK!
THERE'S NOTHING THERE FOR YOU!
NOTHING!!
LET GO—
WHIRL

...!
NO...

YU, WE HAVE TO GO!!
NO!!
YU...
YUICHIRO...
RUN...
WHAP
CATTLE DON'T TALK.
STOP! PLEASE!!
YU, YOU CAN'T!!
NNH...

ZLORP
AAAAAAAAAAHHH!!
WHA...?
FLASH

HUH?
WHAT THE HECK?
HEY, ASURA-MARU.
HM?
OH. HELLO, YU.
WHAT IS IT?
WHAT'S GOING ON HERE?
ARE YOU TRYING TO TAKE OVER MY BODY?
NO.
I'M NOT DOING ANY-THING.
STILL... THIS IS A PROBLEM.

WHO WOULD HAVE THOUGHT THAT I, A DEMON...
...WOULD EVER BE SCARED OF HOW MONSTROUS THE HUMAN I'M POSSESSING COULD BE?
YOU'VE STAINED IT AN UGLY BLACK, SPREADING IT OVER THE WORLD LIKE A CURSE.
YU?
MIKA IS RIGHT.
WHAT'S THAT SUPPOSED TO MEAN?
LOOK AT THE SKY.
IF THERE IS STILL TIME...
...BOTH OF YOU SHOULD RUN AS FAR AWAY FROM HUMANS AS YOU CAN.

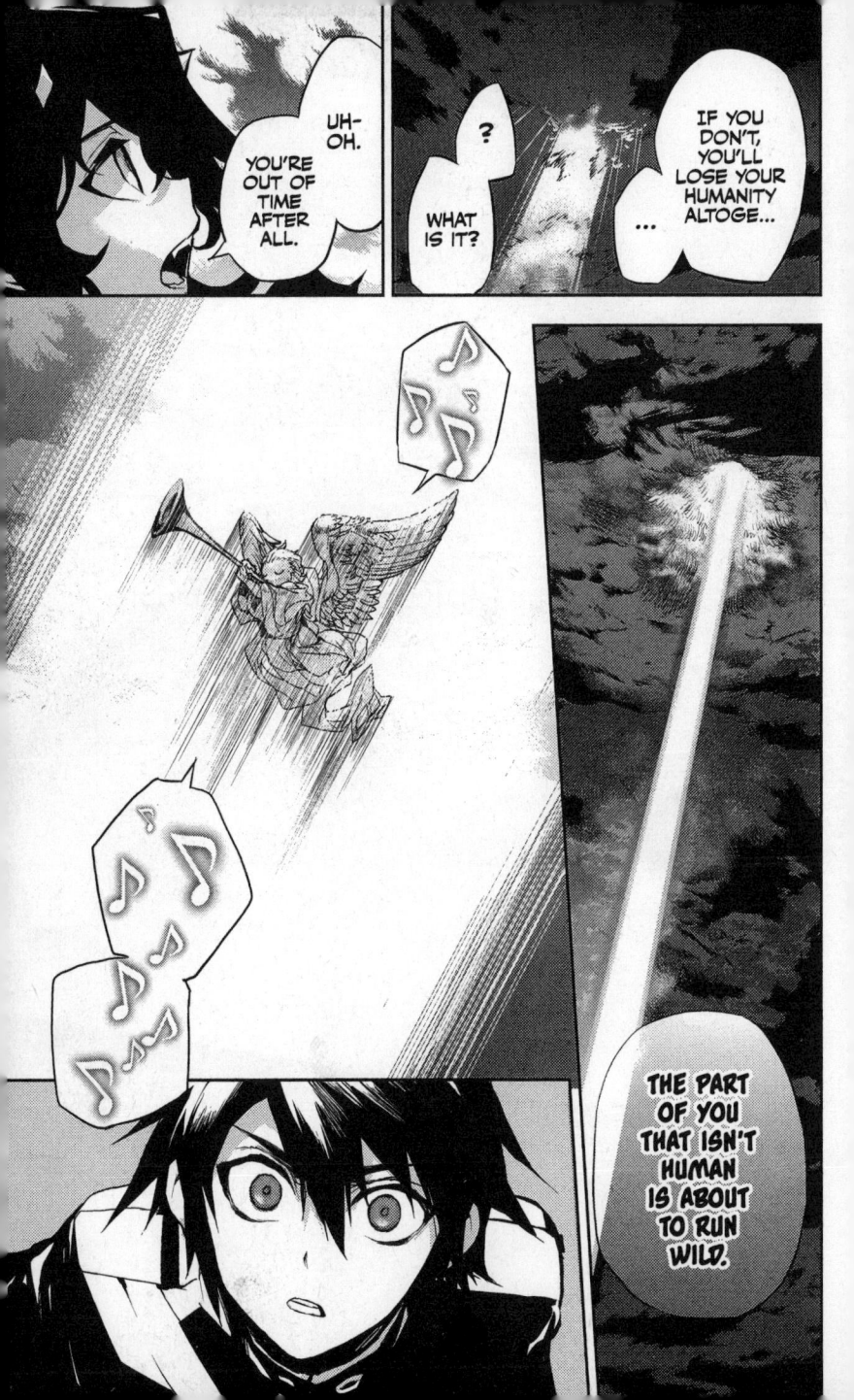
IF YOU DON'T, YOU'LL LOSE YOUR HUMANITY ALTOGE...
...
?
WHAT IS IT?
UH-OH.
YOU'RE OUT OF TIME AFTER ALL.
THE PART OF YOU THAT ISN'T HUMAN IS ABOUT TO RUN WILD.

IT'S BEGUN.

RAAAAAAAOH!!!
I KNEW IT! THOSE HUMANS *DID* DO SOMETHING TO HIM!!

YU, DON'T!
COME WITH ME AND—
WSH
THIMM
...!!
WHAT THE HECK?
LOOKS LIKE SOMETHING DANGEROUS ...

WHAT?
!
GOOD-NESS, WHAT WAS THAT?
HUMANS CERTAINLY KNOW HOW TO CRAFT UNPLEASANT MONSTERS.
SKCH

Hmm ...
LOOKS LIKE TROUBLE.
WHAT NOW, FERID?
WHAT IS THAT THING?
YOU.
SKWEEZ
GOOD QUESTION.
IMPERTINENT HUMAN. IS THIS ANOTHER ONE OF YOUR SPECIAL "EXPERIMENTS," THEN?
WHERE ON EARTH DOES THAT BOTTOMLESS GREED OF YOURS COME FROM?
IT'S FRIGHTENING. TRULY FRIGHTENING.
AND TO TOP IT OFF, YOU NEVER MANAGE TO CONTROL WHAT YOU CREATE.
SEE?

S-S-SSI-SINNERS ...
S-SINNERS MUST... D-DIE.
M-M-MUST KILL... ALL S-SI-SINNERS.

YU!
WHAT...?
DON'T!!
YUICHIRO ...?

Seraph of the End

VAMPIRE REIGN

CHAPTER 14 Everyone's a Sinner

Seraph of the End

VAMPIRE REIGN

S-S-SI...
SSSIN-NERS...
M-MUST K-K-KILL...
...ALL SSSIN-NERS...

HUH?
WH-WHAT ...?
YUICHIRO ...?

THUK

YU, NO!!
DON'T KILL HUMANS!

Y-YOU...!
BUT WHY?

SHUT UP, HUMAN.
I DIDN'T DO THIS FOR YOU.

HOW DARE YOU USE HIM LIKE THIS...!
DAMMIT...
THE WOUND ISN'T HEALING!
DO NOT INTER-FERE, VAMPIRE.
ALL HUMANS MUST BE KILLED.

THUD
FLIK
SHINOA, EMBRACE YU!!
THAT SHOULD BRING HIM BACK FROM WHAT HE'S BECOME!
HUH?
WHAT?
YOU MEAN... HUG HIM?
DMP
Y...
YU-ICHIRO!

GAAA-AAAH!!
PLEASE COME TO YOUR SENSES!!

GURPH !!
THUD
Y-YU-ICHIRO?
YU-ICHIRO!
KOFF
HUMAN BASTARDS ...
WHAT HAVE YOU DONE TO HIM?!
PRETTY FLASHY ENTRANCE, DON'TCHA THINK?
THAT'S MY ACE IN THE HOLE.
HEH HEH HEH...

OH IT DID.
WE WERE JUST DECOYS MEANT TO BUY SOME TIME, AFTER ALL.
BUT IT DIDN'T DO MUCH FOR YOU, DID IT?
WHOOPS, IT LOOKS LIKE THE CAT'S OUT OF THE BAG.
Shinya Hiragi (Major General)

*Ed: Byakkomaru = "White Tiger"

BLAM
BLAM
SH

DAMN!
THMM
THMM
FW
TUP
WHEW! THAT WAS CLOSE.
WITHOUT YOUR OH-SO-COURTEOUS WARNING ...
...
...THAT SHOT MIGHT HAVE KILLED ME.

MY, MY.
LOOK AT THAT.

WELL DONE, LT. COLONEL ICHINOSE.
GOOD JOB FOR A PIECE OF TRASH FROM AN INSIGNIFICANT JUNIOR BRANCH FAMILY.
Kureto Hiragi (Lieutenant General)
SHUT UP.
THE HIRAGI FAMILY WILL TAKE OVER FROM HERE.
MY PEOPLE WILL DESTROY THOSE VAMPIRES FOR YOU.

I'LL MAKE SURE YOU RECEIVE AN APPROPRIATE REWARD LATER.
HA HA! DON'T GRUMBLE, GUREN.
LIKE ALWAYS, STEAL ALL THE GLORY WHILE OTHERS DO ALL THE WORK.
BE MY GUEST.
SHUP
LET'S GO, MEN!
CAPTURE THOSE VAMPIRE NOBLES ALIVE.
...DEFIES THE JAPANESE IMPERIAL DEMON ARMY...
WHOEVER DEFIES HUMANITY ...
...MUST BE TAUGHT A VERY THOROUGH, PAINFUL LESSON.
...THE HIRAGI FAMILY...
...OR DARES DEFY US...

HEY, FERID!
WHAT NOW?
GO FORTH.
SHIFF
HMM...
ALL THESE FILTHY HUMANS CRAWLING ABOUT IS TURNING MY STOMACH.
I'M GOING TO LEAVE.
HA HA... I SEE YOU STILL HAVE NO PRIDE.
WHAT ABOUT ME?
LIVE OR DIE, WHICH-EVER YOU'D LIKE.
AWW! YOU CALL ME OUT HERE AND THAT'S ALL?
Aha ha ha!
What say we both go home, then?
I've done what I wished to do anyway.

HN?
WHAT DID YOU "WISH TO DO"?
THAT'S MY SECRET.
UNTIL NEXT TIME, CROWLEY.
ZWP
...
Pat

COME. IT'S TIME TO RETREAT.
I STILL ...
I STILL HAVE TO RESCUE YU!
LET GO OF ME!
SEE HOW THAT HUMAN GREED IS DRAPED OVER HIM LIKE AN UGLY MANTLE?
LOOK.
OH, I COMPLETELY UNDERSTAND, BUT RIGHT NOW YOU CAN'T.

...!
DAMMIT ...!
grind
DAMN THOSE ...
...FILTHY HUMANS!!

ARE YOU STARTING TO HATE HUMANITY NOW?
AHA HA!
WELL?
YES, I DO HATE HUMANITY.
BUT I HATE VAMPIRES TOO.
Ooh, whatever shall you do?
I CAN HARDLY WAIT TO FIND OUT.
BUT FOR NOW, LET'S GO HOME.
LET ME GO!

THAT WILL BE QUITE ENOUGH OF THAT.
YOU'VE HAD YOUR FUN FOR TODAY.
NOW SHUT YOUR MOUTH LIKE A GOOD BOY.
!!
GRAB
Y...
YU...
TMP

...
WELL.
THAT WENT ABOUT HOW WE EXPECTED.
LET NONE ESCAPE!
KILL EVERY VAMPIRE IN SHINJUKU!
LT. COLONEL GUREN.
I'D LIKE...
...TO ASK YOU A QUESTION LATER.
LT. COLO-NEL?

FORGET ABOUT HIM. HOW'S YU DOING?!
I'M NOT INTERESTED IN ANSWERING.
DON'T BOTHER COMING BY.
HE...
HE LOOKS LIKE HE NEEDS HEALING.
LT. COLONEL!
skf

I'LL CARRY HIM!
LET'S MOVE !!
YES...
HE WILL DEFINITELY REQUIRE HEALING.
LET'S HURRY BACK TO SHINJUKU.
HUP
"MIKA."
"YU."

Five Days Later

Japanese Imperial Demon Army's Shinjuku Barracks
Underground

GA LUNK...
I AM SURE YOU RECOGNIZE THIS UNIFORM...
HALT.
...BUT JUST IN CASE, I AM A SOLDIER OF THE JAPANESE IMPERIAL DEMON ARMY...
...AND A MEMBER OF A VAMPIRE EXTERMINATION UNIT.
THIS AREA IS OFF LIMITS.

I'M AFRAID EVEN VAMPIRE EXTERMI-NATION UNITS CANNOT ENTER.
NO OFFICER UNDER THE RANK OF MAJOR IS PERMITTED.
MAY I ASK WHAT KIND OF PLACE IS BEYOND HERE?
IT'S A LAB FOR EXPERI-MENTING ON OUR GUINEA PIGS.
HEY!!
C'MON, IT DOESN'T MATTER. IT'S COMMON KNOWLEDGE IN SHINJUKU.
GUINEA PIGS?
OF WHAT SORT?

VAMPIRES. WE'RE EXPERIMENTING ON THEM TO FIND ANY EXPLOITABLE WEAK POINTS.
HA!
IF YOU WANNA CALL THOSE THINGS HUMAN, THEN YEAH.
SO, IN OTHER WORDS, THIS IS MORE HUMAN EXPERIMENTATION.
UH, DIDN'T YOU HEAR ME WHEN I SAID NO ONE UNDER MAJOR—
AH WELL.
PLEASE LET ME PASS.
shf

I AM A MEMBER OF THE HIRAGI FAMILY...
THE LEADERS OF THIS DEMON ARMY.
AM I STILL FORBIDDEN TO PASS?
N-NO, MA'AM!
OF COURSE YOU MAY PASS!
THANK YOU.
...
UM... MA'AM ?
MAY I ASK A QUESTION?
WHY IS A MEMBER OF THE GLORIOUS HIRAGI FAMILY...
... OCCUPYING THE LOWLY RANK OF SERGEANT?

BESIDES, I HAVE LITTLE INTEREST IN THE PETTY POWER STRUGGLES OF THE UPPER RANKS.

I LOST MY ELDER SISTER TO THAT SORT OF THING, AFTER ALL.

I LIKE HOW THE WORD ROLLS OFF OF THE TONGUE.

I'LL BE GOING IN THEN.
IF YOU WOULD PLEASE OPEN THE DOOR?
...
Y-YES, MA'AM.

BREEEE

plip
tok
tok
CHUNK

ちょっと
タフ

LT. COLONEL GUREN.
THERE YOU ARE.

I'VE BEEN LOOKING FOR YOU FOR FIVE DAYS.
SIR.
I HAVE A FEW QUESTIONS FOR YOU.
REALLY.
GOOD FOR YOU.
GO HOME—
AND I DON'T HAVE ANY ANSWERS FOR YOU.
YUICHIRO HAS YET TO WAKE UP.

WHAT DID YOU DO TO HIM, LT. COLONEL?
NO...
WHAT ARE YOU TRYING TO DO TO HIM?
Shf
KLATTER

WHAT WAS THAT THING HE TURNED INTO ON THE BATTLE-FIELD?
ANSWER ME, LT. COLONEL GUREN.
YOU TOLD ME THAT BECAUSE BLACK DEMON SERIES WEAPONS ARE UNIQUE...
...THAT HE WAS TO BE GIVEN A UNIQUE SUPPLE-MENT.
I DID AS YOU ORDERED.
HA HA!
LOOK AT YOU, ACTUALLY GETTING EMOTIONAL FOR ONCE.
ARE YOU MAD AT ME?
WAS THAT WHAT CAUSED HIM TO GO BERSERK?
SO, WHAT'S THE ANSWER YOU WANT TO HEAR?

IF I TOLD YOU I DIDN'T DO ANYTHING, WOULD THAT MAKE YOU FEEL BETTER?
RIDICU-LOUS!
THERE'S NO WAY THAT'S THE CASE—
SO THEN, IF I TOLD YOU WE'RE USING HIM IN OUR EXPERIMENTS, WOULD YOU BE ANGRY?
HUMANS ARE WEAK. FRAGILE.
NOW THAT THE WORLD HAS ENDED, WHAT DO WE HAVE TO DO TO SURVIVE?

YOUR SISTER, MAHIRU HIRAGI, INVENTED CURSED GEAR.
WHAT DO WE HAVE TO DO TO KILL VAMPIRES?
TO ERADICATE THE HORSEMEN?
WITHOUT IT...

HOW MANY PEOPLE WERE SACRIFICED IN *THAT* LONG PROCESS?
I...
...DO YOU HONESTLY THINK HUMANITY WOULD BE ABLE TO SURVIVE?

UNDERSTAND? SO QUIT SPEWING IDEALISTIC CRAP AT ME, LITTLE GIRL.

OR, WHAT...
ARE YOU FALLING IN LOVE WITH YU?

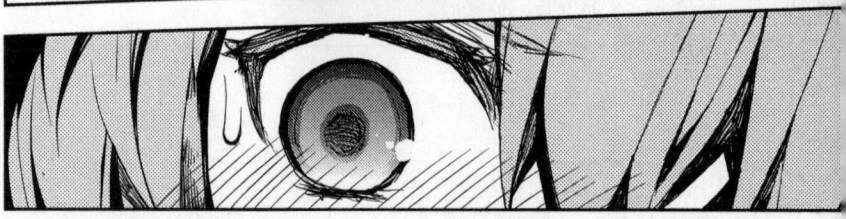

WHA...
HA HA HA! LOOK AT YOUR FACE.
AH, WELL. I COULDN'T CARE LESS HOW YOU TWO FEEL ABOUT EACH OTHER.
I DON'T NEED YOU TO COME UPDATE ME ON YOUR LITTLE CRUSHES.
LEAVE.
SIR, WAIT!
WHIRL
YOU HAVEN'T ANSWERED–
LEAVE.
...
RGH ....!
OH, ONE THING.

CONSIDER PAYING HIM A VISIT.

YUICHIRO.
PLEASE WAKE UP SOON.
YUICHIRO ...?
...
AHA HA...
NEVER.
ME? IN LOVE?

shff
WAKE UP SOON, YUICHIRO.
BUT...
PLEASE.

Seraph of the End

VAMPIRE REIGN

CHAPTER 15
Complicated Connections

Chapter 15
Complicated Connections

BEEEP
CURSE DETOX-IFICATION COMPLETE.
PSHHH
...
SHOO
SHOO
SHF
!
TEARS ...?
I HAVEN'T CRIED SINCE I BECAME A VAMPIRE...

BEEEP PSHHT
SHEESH!
FOR A BUNCH OF WORTHLESS HUMANS, THEY SURE GAVE US A BEATING.
HOW'RE YOU HOLDING UP, MIKA?
YOU HAD IT THE WORST.

HA!
SO THE NEW RECRUIT STILL HAS THE GUTS TO IGNORE HIS ELDERS?
MORE IMPORTANTLY ...
THAT MONSTER THE HUMANS UNLEASHED ON THE BATTLEFIELD ...
...WHAT WAS IT?
OH, THAT?
I HEAR IT'S TROUBLING EVEN THE PROGENITOR COUNCIL.
IT IS?

SOMETHING LIKE THE "SERAPH OF THE END"?

THOSE HUMANS...
THEY'RE PERFORMING FORBIDDEN RESEARCH THAT COULD END UP DESTROYING THE WORLD.
WHAT WAS IT CALLED AGAIN...?

I HEARD OUR ATTACK ON SHINJUKU ...
...WAS ACTUALLY AIMED AT GETTING WHATEVER *THAT* IS.
REALLY? THEN WE FAILED TO ACHIEVE OUR OBJECTIVE?

WHO KNOWS.
LORD FERID WAS IN CHARGE, AND WHO CAN GUESS WHAT THAT GUY IS THINKING.
SO WHO CAN TELL IF WE SUCCEEDED OR NOT?

BUT...
IF ANYBODY KNOWS ABOUT THAT MONSTER, IT'D BE *YOU*.
MIKA.

I MEAN, THAT MONSTER ...
...WAS SOME HUMAN YOU USED TO KNOW, RIGHT?
IS THAT WHY LADY KRUL FAVORS YOU?
...
IF YOU DON'T WANNA ANSWER, WE'VE GOT PLENTY OF WAYS TO FIND OUT.
MIKAELA HYAKUYA.
WHAT ARE YOU?

YOU WANT TO KNOW...
...WHAT I AM?
YOU MAKE IT SOUND ...
...LIKE YOU AREN'T HUMAN ANYMORE ...
ALL YOU HAVE TO DO IS LOOK AT ME.
THAT'S EASY.
tak

I'M JUST AN UGLY BLOOD-SUCKER.
ZZZT
WHAT'S WITH *THAT* ANSWER?

...TO THE ROYAL AUDIENCE CHAMBER.
YOU'D BETTER GET GOING, QUEEN'S PET.
HEH. LOOKS LIKE SHE'S CALLING FOR YOU.
ATTEN-TION.
ATTEN-TION.
MIKAELA HYAKUYA.
YOU HAVE BEEN SUMMONED BY THIRD PROGENITOR KRUL TEPES.
PROCEED AT ONCE...

MMH...

Shff

ZZZZ
ZZZZ
WHERE AM I?
LAST I REMEMBER, I WAS IN SHINJUKU ...

PLEASE, YU! DON'T LOOK BACK!
THERE'S NOTHING THERE FOR YOU!
NOTHING !!

HEY, YOICHI! WAKE UP!
SNAK
WHAT THE HECK IS GOING ON HERE?!
NH...

OH RIGHT!
BLOOD-SUCKERS GOT EVERY-ONE!
WAIT, HUH? HOW COME I'M STILL ALIVE?

OW... THAT HURT...

YUICHIRO!
YOU'RE FINALLY AWAKE!
THAT'S MY LINE!
NOW TELL ME, WHAT HAPPENED BACK AT—
HUG
H-hey! I asked you a—
tup tup
I NEED TO TELL EVERYONE RIGHT AWAY!
WE WERE ALL SUPER WORRIED ABOUT YOU!
I'LL GO GET EVERY-BODY RIGHT NOW!
Hold on! Answer my question first!

...
JUST ONE THING!
HOW IS EVERY-ONE?!
ARE THEY ALL OKAY?!
What, you were worried about us?
peek
Yeah! Duh!
RELAX THEN.
YOU WERE THE ONLY ONE WHO GOT HURT REALLY BAD.
REALLY?
whew
BUT YOU WERE IN A COMA FOR A WEEK.
EVERY-ONE WAS REALLY, REALLY WORRIED!
A WEEK? SERIOUSLY?

I'M GONNA TELL EVERYONE YOU'RE AWAKE.
YEAH!

ALL OF THEM.
THEY'RE ALL FINE.
THAT'S GOOD.

...
THEY'RE OKAY.

MIKA...

FORGET ABOUT ALL OF THEM AND RUN AWAY WITH ME!

IT WASN'T A DREAM.

AND THAT MEANS MIKA REALLY IS ALIVE.

HA HA... HE'S ALIVE...

HA HA HA...

I'M NOT DREAMING ...

HE REALLY DIDN'T DIE...

THANK GOD...
I'M SO GLAD...!

EXCUSE ME.
IS THIS THE CRYBABY'S ROOM?
blink
Look at that face.
You're a mess!
smirk
Dwah !!
N-no, this isn't what you think...!
AHA HA! IT'S NO BIG DEAL, REALLY.
ANYONE WOULD CRY.

ME, I'M JUST GLAD...
...THAT YOU FINALLY DECIDED TO WAKE UP.
AFTER ALL, YOU JUST LEARNED A FAMILY MEMBER IS STILL ALIVE.
SO WHAT HAPPENED OUT THERE?

I SEE...
NOPE.
YOU DON'T REMEMBER AT ALL?
I, UH... DON'T REMEMBER AFTER PARTWAY THROUGH...
WELL.
BECAUSE THAT'S WHEN YOU SAID YOU WERE SLEEPY AND CURLED UP FOR A NAP.
...
WHAT TRULY HAPPENED ...
Wha ?!
N-no way, I didn't ...
OF COURSE NOT.
...BUT REINFORCE-MENTS ARRIVED.
OUR ENTIRE SQUAD WAS IN DANGER OF BEING WIPED OUT...
...WAS YOU SUDDENLY COLLAPSED.

NOT JUST ANY REIN-FORCEMENTS, EITHER. LT. GENERAL KURETO HIRAGI...
STILL, OVER HALF OF THEIR TOTAL NUMBERS ESCAPED.
WE WERE ABLE TO KILL QUITE A FEW OF THE NON-NOBLE VAMPIRES, YES.
WE EVEN CAPTURED A HANDFUL.
THEN ALL THE BLOOD-SUCKERS WERE KILLED?!

...AND MAJOR GENERAL SHINYA HIRAGI...
...ARRIVED WITH THE SHIBUYA MAIN ARMY.
YOU'RE CURIOUS ABOUT MIKA'S FATE, YES?
THEN ...
WAS, UM...

SO HE'S NOT DEAD?
NO.
UNFORTUNATELY, HE MANAGED TO ESCAPE.
WELL, ER...
BUT...
...YOU SAID HE GOT AWAY, RIGHT?
SO HE LEFT ME BEHIND AND RAN AWAY...?
YOU DON'T HAVE TO SUGAR-COAT IT FOR ME.
I DON'T CARE IF MIKA'S OUR ENEMY OR OUR ALLY.
AS LONG AS HE'S ALIVE, I'M HAPPY.
SO... JUST TELL ME THE TRUTH.

THIS IS A LITTLE DIFFICULT TO SAY...
...AS I DON'T WANT TO OVER-EXCITE A SICK PERSON.
MIKA WAS OBVIOUSLY GREATLY WORRIED ABOUT YOU AND WOULDN'T LEAVE...
...UNTIL ANOTHER VAMPIRE PHYSICALLY DRAGGED HIM AWAY.
REALLY?
YES.
OKAY.
THANKS.

HAVING SAID THAT...
I WOULD RATHER YOU NOT SNEAK OUT OF THE HOSPITAL AND INTO THE VAMPIRE CAPITAL IN AN ATTEMPT TO RESCUE HIM.
HUH?
OH!

NO, I WON'T.
I'M NOT THAT STUPID.
ESPECIALLY WITH YOU AND YOICHI SO WORRIED OVER ME AND STUFF.
FOR NOW, JUST KNOWING HE'S ALIVE IS ENOUGH FOR ME.
I SEE.
THAT'S GOOD.
YEAH.
HEY, SHINOA ?
YES?
THANKS FOR WORRYING ABOUT ME.
...

YOU'RE WELCOME.
HEY, YOUR NECK.
HM?
SWIP
WHA? W-WAIT!
ARE YOU OKAY? THE BITE DOESN'T HURT, DOES IT?

O-OH, ER...
THAT?
bump bump
IT'S, UH... FINE.
THE VAMPIRE ONLY TOOK A LITTLE SIP, THAT'S ALL...
SLAM
Yo! Block-head Yu!
It's about time you woke up!
HUH?

I WAS JUST SHOWING YU WHERE I WAS BITTEN.
WH-WHAT THE HECK ARE YOU TWO DOING?!
WAIT, YOU'VE GOT BANDAGES TOO!
ARE YOU OKAY?!
HUH?
NO NO NO!
WE, AH...
HUH? OH...
SO THAT'S ALL IT WAS.
I, UM...
GRAB
SHUT YOUR TRAPS, WE'RE IN A HOSPITAL.

Excuse me?!
HUNH. YOU'RE ACTUALLY LOOKING KINDA OKAY, YU.
YEAH. SORRY FOR MAKING YOU WORRY.
HUH?
WHY THE HELL WOULD I BE WORRIED ABOUT A MORON LIKE YOU?
OR SO HE SAYS.
EVEN THOUGH HE CARED FOR YOU WITH SUCH LOVING TENDERNESS WHILE YOU WERE UNCONSCIOUS.
H-HEY!!
GAH
HA HA HA.
HEY, UM, GUYS?
LISTEN A SEC.

whew
HN?
WHAT IS IT?
THANKS.
I'M SORRY I MADE YOU ALL WORRY.
OKAY.
YES?

AND I'M REALLY GLAD EVERYONE SURVIVED.
I'VE BEEN BLESSED WITH GREAT FRIENDS.

WHOA, WHOA. ARE WE SURE THE DOCTOR SHOULDN'T COME SEE HIM AGAIN?
OH, COME ON, GUYS! YUICHIRO'S ALWAYS BEEN A NICE GUY.
WHAT ULTERIOR MOTIVES IS THIS "NICE GUY" ACT COVERING UP?
YEAH, HE'S OBVIOUSLY HIT HIS HEAD A FEW TIMES.
YOU ALL WANNA GET THROWN OUT THE WINDOW?

LEAVE ?

SINCE WE WERE ON THE FRONT LINES, WE'VE BEEN GIVEN SOME LEAVE.
WHATEVER. STAY HERE AND REST, GOT THAT?

YES.
SHINOA SQUAD IS OFFICIALLY ON LEAVE UNTIL YOU'RE BACK ON YOUR FEET.
REALLY ?
LEAVE, EH...?
I GUESS I COULD OBEY ORDERS AND REST. JUST THIS ONCE.
I DON'T WANT TO CAUSE ANY MORE TROUBLE THAN I ALREADY HAVE.
...
BESIDES, I DO FEEL KINDA TIRED.
WELL, GOOD.
I'LL GO GET US SOMETHING TO DRINK.
I'LL HELP!

WONDERFUL! KIMIZUKI'S EXPERIENCE CARING FOR HIS HOSPITAL-BOUND SISTER SHINES THROUGH.
ON THE OTHER HAND, FOR A GIRL, YOU'RE STANDING AROUND LIKE AN INSENSITIVE LUMP, MITSU.
YOU'RE A GIRL AND YOU AREN'T DOING ANYTHING EITHER, SHINOA!
Aha ha! But the squad leader doesn't have to do anything!♪
Ha ha ha
NONE OF MY NEW FRIENDS DIED.
AND MIKA'S ALIVE.
WHAT THE HECK?
IS IT REALLY OKAY FOR GOOD THINGS TO HAPPEN TO ME?

JUST YOU WAIT, MIKA.
I SWEAR...
ANY-WAY.
HE'S ALIVE, AND THAT MEANS I STILL HAVE A CHANCE.

...
...!
I PROMISE...
JUST YOU WAIT, YU.

I'LL SAVE YOU.

I'LL SAVE YOU.

Mean-
while
HUMANITY'S ALL-CONSUMING GREED CONTINUES TO EXPAND UNCHECKED...

GWOOO O
OOOOO
HA HA! GOOD-NESS...
EVERYTHING IS PROCEEDING SO PERFECTLY IT'S ALMOST LAUGHABLE!
...AND VAMPIRES' BOUNDLESS ARROGANCE HAS THEM LOOKING DOWN THEIR NOSES AT THE ENTIRE WORLD.
DON'T YOU AGREE?

MY EVER-SO-AMUSING PARTNER.
HERE YOU GO.

Seraph of the End: Vampire Reign 4 / **END**

HELLO, I'M TAKAYA KAGAMI. HERE'S THE FOURTH INSTALLMENT. HOPE YOU LIKE IT!

MITSUBA SANGU

As a daughter of the prestigious Sangu Family, she is an elite warrior. She has an older sister who is the same age as Guren, and was even his classmate in high school. Yes, as you would expect, Mitsuba's sister is a prominent character in the story detailing the world before its end—the light novel *Seraph of the End: Guren Ichinose's Catastrophe at 16*.

Mitsuba is a second daughter, but her name means "three-leaf clover." Her older sister is named "Aoi," which is the name of a two-leafed species of wild ginger. What on earth were their parents thinking when they named them? Who knows. Oh, Aoi will probably appear in the manga starting somewhere in volume 5, so keep an eye out!

SHINOA: "MY, WE BOTH HAVE HIGHLY TALENTED OLDER SISTERS? WE BECOME MORE AND MORE ALIKE EVERY DAY!"

MITSUBA: "YOU'RE THE LAST PERSON I WANT TO BE ANYTHING LIKE!!"

SHINOA: "OH, COME. NO NEED TO BE SHY! AFTER ALL, WE'RE SO CLOSE WE BATHE TOGETHER."

MITSUBA: "WE DO NOT! YOU JUST BUTT INTO MY SHOWERS!!"

Mitsuba's weapon is an enormous axe. Before serialization for this series began, I remember talking with Mr. Yamamoto on the train about how much we loved girls who wield huge axes.

Mitsuba's big sister in high school, eight years ago.

ASURAMARU

This is the demon Yu made his contract with. He lives inside Yu's sword. He's also shrouded in mystery. We have quite a lot set up for his character, but most of it is still secret. Believe it or not, Asuramaru is connected to Guren, and makes a brief cameo in the third volume of the novel. Oh! And eight-year-old Yu also has a cameo. Look for it! How will Yu's and Asuramaru's destinies intertwine? Also...

Demons.
Vampires.
Devils.
Angels.

All of these and the truths behind them will soon begin to pop up in the manga. I hope you're looking forward to it!

ASURAMARU: "YOU DON'T NEED TO BOTHER TELLING ANYTHING ABOUT ME, ACTUALLY. I'M FINE STAYING SECRETIVE. DON'T YOU AGREE, SHI?"

SHIKAMA DOJI: "..."

In case you don't remember, Shikama Doji is the demon who lives inside Shinoa's scythe. Shi first appeared in chapter 3. Both Shi and Asuramaru are still both big unknowns!

Shikama Doji

Afterword

HELLO. I'M TAKAYA KAGAMI. HOW DID YOU LIKE *SERAPH OF THE END: VAMPIRE REIGN* VOLUME 4? I CONSIDER THIS VOLUME THE FIRST MAJOR CLIMAX OF THE SERIES. I MEAN, THERE WAS WHAT HAPPENED BETWEEN YU AND MIKA! ALSO, UNTIL NOW WE KEPT MOST OF THE WORLD-BUILDING LOW-KEY SO THAT READERS COULD GET TO KNOW THE CHARACTERS FIRST. NOW WE WILL START EXPLORING MORE OF THE WORLD ITSELF.

TO BE HONEST, WE HAVE OVER 100 PAGES WRITTEN ON JUST THE SETTING ITSELF (AFTER ALL, WE NEEDED BACKGROUND FOR BOTH THE NOVEL AND THE MANGA). WE'VE BEEN RELEASING TIDBITS SO FAR SO AS NOT TO CONFUSE ANYBODY. BUT NOW THAT EVERYTHING IS IN PLACE, IT'S TIME TO START SHOWING OFF MORE OF THE WORLD!

ON ANOTHER NOTE, I'VE STARTED TO REALLY APPRECIATE HOW WE'VE BEEN DETAILING THE WORLD OF EIGHT YEARS AGO IN THE NOVEL AND LEFT THE WORLD OF TODAY, THE RUINED WORLD, TO THE MANGA. I'VE WORKED ON VARIOUS TYPES OF STORIES, BUT GETTING TO WRITE BOTH A STORY'S PAST AND ITS PRESENT AS THEIR OWN WHOLE WORKS IS REALLY SOMETHING ELSE. NOT ONLY DO YOU GET TO BOIL DOWN THE SETTING TO THE REAL NITTY-GRITTY DETAILS, EACH WORK CAN HAVE SERIOUS INFLUENCE ON THE OTHER.

FOR EXAMPLE, IF SOMETHING MAJOR HAPPENS IN THE NOVEL'S PAST TIMELINE, IT CAN GROW AND EXPAND—IN MY HEAD, AT LEAST—AND MAYBE HAVE SOME BIG REPERCUSSIONS ON THE MANGA'S PRESENT TIMELINE. CONVERSELY, THERE ARE TIMES WHERE I WIND UP THINKING, "AW, MAN! IF I WRITE THAT IN THE NOVEL, I'M GONNA HAVE TO REDO ALL OF THE MANGA SCRIPTS I WORKED ON AHEAD OF TIME!"

HOWEVER, I STILL CONSIDER MYSELF BLESSED WITH AN INTERESTING STORY AND FUN COMRADES (MR. YAMAMOTO, MR. FURUYA, MY EDITORS FROM SHUEISHA AND KODANSHA, AND ALL MY READERS!) IT IS WITH A HAPPY HEART THAT I GO ON...TO DO BATTLE WITH MORE DEADLINES. *UGH.* BUT THANK YOU!

SPEAKING OF THANKING PEOPLE... I SEEM TO REMEMBER GETTING A BIG TWO-PAGE SPREAD AD FOR *SERAPH OF THE END* IN ONE OF THE OTHER STORIES I'M WORKING ON, *THE LEGEND OF THE LEGENDARY HEROES*. NOW MY EDITOR FOR THAT TITLE IS STARTING TO ASK ME WHEN WE'RE GOING TO DO AN AD FOR *LOTLH* HERE, AND I DID PROMISE HIM I WOULD... BUT I DON'T HAVE THE PAGE SPACE THIS TIME EITHER!

SO, RIGHT HERE, RIGHT NOW I'M GOING TO MENTION THAT I'VE STARTED ANOTHER NEW SERIES, *APOCALYPSE ALICE* (PUBLISHED BY FANTASIA BUNKO / FUJIMI SHOBO)! FOR THOSE OF YOU WHO HAVE READ *SERAPH OF THE END* AND CAN'T GET ENOUGH, PLEASE CONSIDER PICKING UP *APOCALYPSE ALICE*! :D

NOW THAT I'VE PLUGGED ANOTHER OF MY SERIES FOR A TOTALLY DIFFERENT PUBLISHER, LET ME REMIND YOU THAT AT THE END OF THE MONTH, VOLUME 3 OF *SERAPH OF THE END: GUREN ICHINOSE'S CATASTROPHE AT 16* COMES OUT. EIGHT-YEAR-OLD YU APPEARS, AND THE WORLD FINALLY BEGINS ITS SLIDE INTO DISASTER. I HOPE YOU LIKE IT!

TAKAYA KAGAMI

A brilliant sketch of Yuichiro by the author!

TAKAYA KAGAMI is a prolific light novelist whose works include the action and fantasy series *The Legend of the Legendary Heroes*, which has been adapted into manga, anime and a video game. His previous series, *A Dark Rabbit Has Seven Lives*, also spawned a manga and anime series.

"My desk with the tiltable top finally arrived, and the tendonitis I've been suffering from scribbling too much has suddenly subsided! A new era has begun, everyone! I hope you enjoy *Seraph of the End: Vampire Reign* volume 4 and *Seraph of the End: Guren Ichinose's Catastrophe at 16* volume 3, coming soon!"

YAMATO YAMAMOTO, born 1983, is an artist and illustrator whose works include the *Kure-nai* manga and the light novels *Kure-nai*, *9S -Nine S-* and *Denpa Teki na Kanojo*. Both *Denpa Teki na Kanojo* and *Kure-nai* have been adapted into anime.

"Yu and Mika finally meet. What trials await the pair now? I hope you enjoy it."

DAISUKE FURUYA previously assisted Yamato Yamamoto with storyboards for *Kure-nai*.

VIZMANGA

Read manga anytime, anywhere!

From our newest hit series to the classics you know and love, the best manga in the world is now available digitally. Buy a volume* of digital manga for your:

- iOS device (**iPad®, iPhone®, iPod® touch**) through the **VIZ Manga app**
- Android-powered device (**phone or tablet**) with a browser by visiting VIZManga.com
- **Mac or PC computer** by visiting VIZManga.com

VIZ Digital has loads to offer:

- 500+ ready-to-read volumes
- New volumes each week
- FREE previews
- Access on multiple devices! Create a log-in through the app so you buy a book once, and read it on your device of choice!*

To learn more, visit www.viz.com/apps

*** Some series may not be available for multiple devices. Check the app on your device to find out what's available.**

DEATH NOTE © 2003 by Tsugumi Ohba, Takeshi Obata/SHUEISHA Inc.
NURARIHYON NO MAGO © 2008 by Hiroshi Shiibashi/SHUEISHA Inc.
ONE PIECE © 1997 by Eiichiro Oda/SHUEISHA Inc.

viz.com/apps

YOU'RE READING THE WRONG WAY!

SERAPH OF THE END reads from right to left, starting in the upper-right corner. Japanese is read from right to left, meaning that action, sound effects, and word-balloon order are completely reversed from English order.

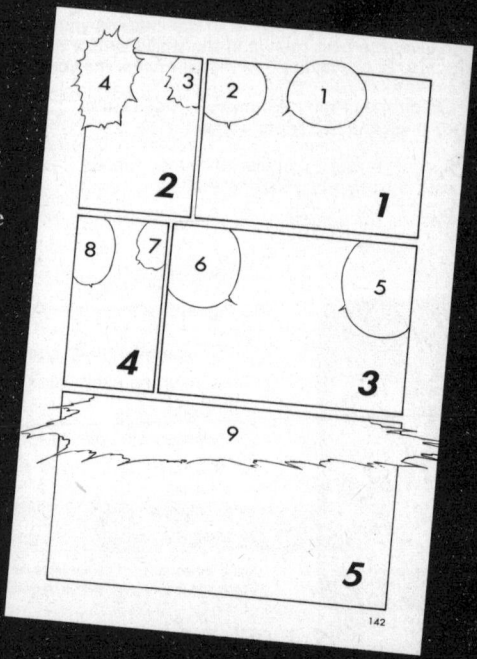

Seraph of the End
VAMPIRE REIGN

VOLUME 4

SHONEN JUMP ADVANCED MANGA EDITION

STORY BY **TAKAYA KAGAMI**
ART BY **YAMATO YAMAMOTO**
STORYBOARDS BY **DAISUKE FURUYA**

TRANSLATION **Adrienne Beck**
TOUCH-UP ART & LETTERING **Sabrina Heep**
DESIGN **Shawn Carrico**
EDITOR **Hope Donovan**

OWARI NO SERAPH © 2012 by Takaya Kagami,
Yamato Yamamoto, Daisuke Furuya
All rights reserved. First published in Japan in 2012 by SHUEISHA Inc., Tokyo.
English translation rights arranged by SHUEISHA Inc.

The stories, characters and incidents mentioned in this publication are entirely fictional.

No portion of this book may be reproduced or transmitted in any form or by any means without written permission from the copyright holders.

Printed in the U.S.A.

Published by VIZ Media, LLC
P.O. Box 77010
San Francisco, CA 94107

10 9 8 7 6 5 4 3 2 1
First printing, March 2015

www.viz.com

www.shonenjump.com

BLUE EXORCIST

STORY AND ART BY KAZUE KATO

RAISED BY FATHER FUJIMOTO, A FAMOUS EXORCIST, RIN OKUMURA NEVER KNEW HIS REAL FATHER. ONE DAY A FATEFUL ARGUMENT WITH FATHER FUJIMOTO FORCES RIN TO FACE A TERRIBLE TRUTH—THE BLOOD OF THE DEMON LORD SATAN RUNS IN RIN'S VEINS!

RIN SWEARS TO DEFEAT SATAN, BUT DOING THAT MEANS ENTERING THE MYSTERIOUS TRUE CROSS ACADEMY AND BECOMING AN EXORCIST HIMSELF!

CATCH UP WITH ALL THE ACTION, DRAMA, COMEDY AND INTRIGUE IN GRAPHIC NOVELS

AVAILABLE NOW!

ONLY $9.99 US / $12.99 CAN EACH!

VOL. 1 ISBN: 978-1-4215-4032-0
VOL. 2 ISBN: 978-1-4215-4033-7
VOL. 3 ISBN: 978-1-4215-4034-4
VOL. 4 ISBN: 978-1-4215-4047-4
VOL. 5 ISBN: 978-1-4215-4076-4
VOL. 6 ISBN: 978-1-4215-4174-7
VOL. 7 ISBN: 978-1-4215-4262-1

WATCH FULL-EPISODES OF THE ANIME FOR FREE ON VIZANIME.COM!

www.viz.com

O NO EXORCIST © 2009 by Kazue Kato/SHUEISHA Inc.